WONDERFUL WORLD OF
SPACE

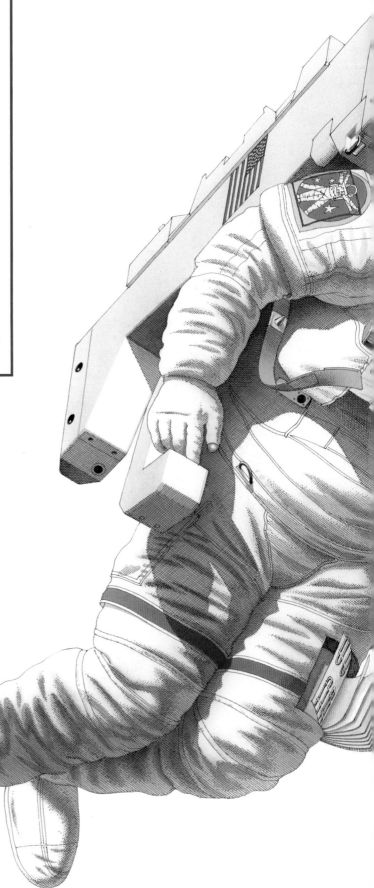

As a 2008 Milken Educator, I take the challenge of reviewing educational materials seriously. As I examined the Disney Learning series, I was impressed by the vivid graphics, captivating content, and introductory humor provided by the various Disney characters. But I decided I should take the material to the true experts, my third grade students, and listen to what they had to say. In their words, "The series is interesting. The books are really fun and eye-catching! They make me want to learn more. I can't wait until the books are in the bookstore!" They looked forward to receiving a new book from the series with as much anticipation as a birthday present or a holiday gift. Based on their expert opinion, this series will be a part of my classroom library. I may even purchase two sets to meet their demand.

Barbara Black
2008 Milken Educator
National Board Certified Teacher—Middle Childhood Generalist
Certified 2001/Renewed 2010

For information address Disney Press,
114 Fifth Avenue, New York, New York 10011-5690.

Visit www.disneybooks.com
Printed in China
ISBN 978-1-4231-4973-6

T425-2382-5-12153
First Edition
Written by Thea Feldman
Fact-checked by Joseph Rao and
Barbara Berliner
All rights reserved.

CONTENTS

WELCOME TO THE
WONDERFUL WORLD OF
SPACE

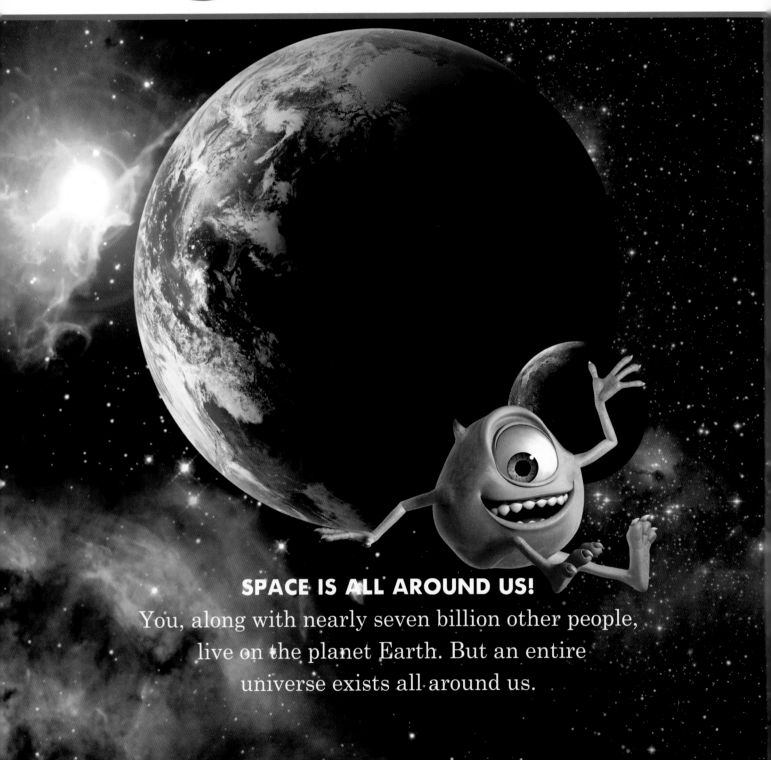

SPACE IS ALL AROUND US!

You, along with nearly seven billion other people, live on the planet Earth. But an entire universe exists all around us.

THE EARTH AND BEYOND

People on Earth have always known that our planet is part of something larger. We can see the Sun, the moon, and the stars in the sky. Sometimes we can even see other planets.

For a long time, though, people believed that Earth was the center of all the action. They thought the Sun and all the other planets revolved around it. But we eventually realized that Earth is just one planet in a solar system.

SOLAR SYSTEMS AND GALAXIES

A solar system literally means "system involving the Sun." It contains planets, moons, asteroids, comets, stars, and anything else floating out there. Ours is trillions of miles wide! That may sound huge, but it's just a small part of a bigger star-packed galaxy, the Milky Way galaxy.

Our Milky Way is not the only galaxy out there. All of them, in turn, are part of the universe. The universe is *it*—the biggest thing there is! It contains absolutely everything—including you.

THE BIG BANG

Scientists don't think the universe was always here. They came up with an explanation called the "Big Bang theory." In it, the universe came from a tiny speck about 13.7 billion years ago. This speck was packed so tightly together and grew so hot that it just exploded! Out of that explosion, the universe and everything in it was born. The universe began growing fast. It's still growing today!

As the universe expands, so does our knowledge of all things in it. Let's take a look at the wonderful world of space.

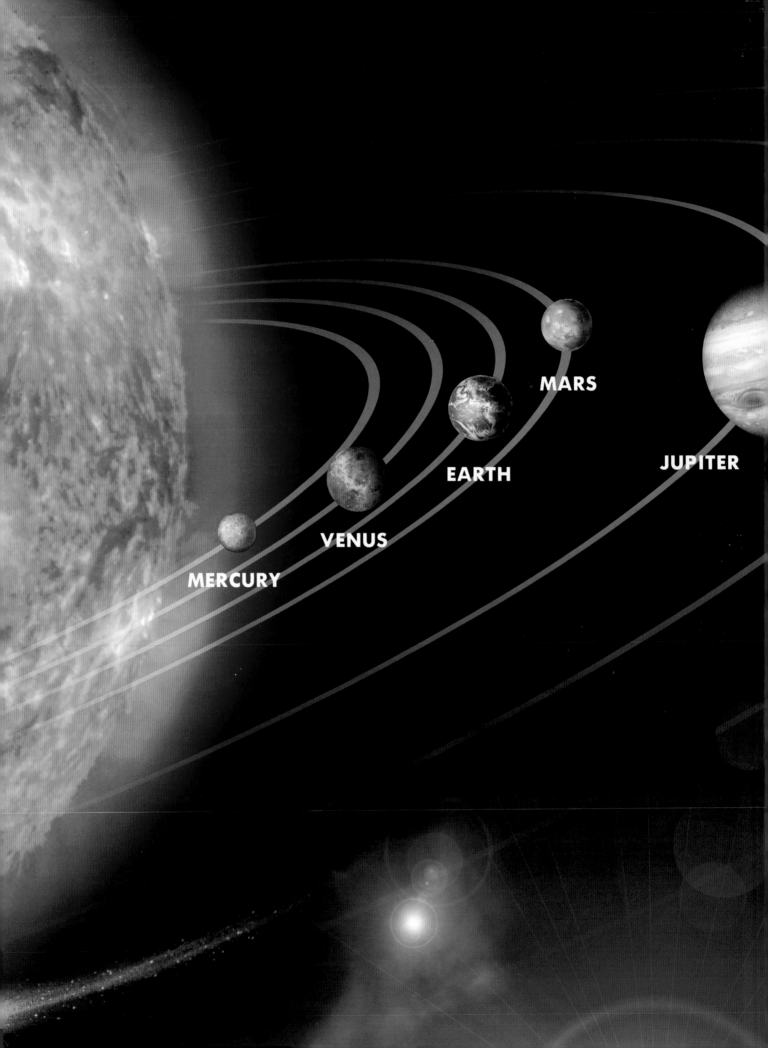

NEPTUNE

URANUS

SATURN

LET'S DISCOVER
PLANETS

Our solar system includes eight planets that revolve around the Sun. So what exactly is a planet? The International Astronomical Union defines a planet as an object orbiting the Sun that's big enough for gravity to give it a round shape. This invisible force pulls objects toward one another. Also, a planet orbits the Sun in its own clear path.

Here's a look at the eight planets and some other interesting objects in our solar system.

MERCURY

Mercury is the planet closest to the Sun. But "closest" isn't what you think—Mercury is still 36 million miles away from the Sun!

Gawrsh, if I went to Mercury, I'd get mighty thirsty!

Mercury is the smallest planet in our solar system, measuring about 3,000 miles wide.

Illustration of Mercury and the Mercury Planetary Orbiter

Mercury's surface (illustration)

HOW HOT
DOES IT GET ON MERCURY?

Because it's so close to the Sun, **Mercury** gets really hot and stays that way. Daytime temperatures there can reach 800°F! But at night, temperatures can dip to -297°F! Mercury is a little planet with big **temperature extremes.** No other planet in our solar system has such extremes.

WHAT DOES THE **SURFACE** OF MERCURY LOOK LIKE?

Mercury looks a lot like Earth's **moon.** The surface has flat plains, steep cliffs, and lots of deep craters. Craters form when rocks and other objects **hurtle** through space and smash into Mercury's surface. The biggest crater on Mercury is the Caloris Basin at 840 miles wide. That's longer than the California coastline in the United States! Inside the **Caloris Basin** are many other, smaller craters.

HOW LONG IS A DAY
ON MERCURY?

Mercury takes 59 days to turn once on its axis. But it takes 88 whole days for the planet to make the trip around the Sun. So Mercury's surface spends 88 days in the Sun and 88 days in darkness. **Nights** can get really **cold!**

If you were standing on Mercury when it reaches the point in its orbit that's closest to the Sun, a weird thing would happen. The Sun seems to stop briefly and move **backwards!**

Two impact craters in Mercury's Caloris Basin

VENUS

Venus is the next closest planet to the Sun. It's also one of Earth's nearest neighbors. But you wouldn't want to go to this neighbor's house! Venus's atmosphere is mostly carbon dioxide, so you can't breathe the air.

That Venus is hot stuff!

Much of Venus's surface is covered in hardened lava from eruptions that happened millions of years ago.

Surface of Venus, volcano and lava flow

WHY DOES IT GET SO HOT ON VENUS?

Day or night, the temperature on **Venus** hovers around 860°F. It's the hottest planet in our solar system. Venus's **atmosphere** is very thick, with lots of heavy clouds. The Sun's heat filters through and warms the planet. But all that carbon dioxide traps the Sun's heat near the planet's surface, where it builds up. This is called the "**greenhouse effect**."

Venus

Lightning in Venus's clouds

WHAT ARE VENUS'S CLOUDS MADE OF?

Venus's atmosphere is a heavy blanket of carbon dioxide. The thick, yellowish clouds are made up of **sulfur dioxide.** It combines with water vapor to make the thick atmosphere. The sulfur dioxide comes from volcanoes! Venus has more **volcanoes** than any other planet. So many volcanoes means that lots of lava has flowed onto the planet's surface and lots of ash—containing sulfur dioxide—has been **spewed** into the air.

WHAT OTHER THINGS ARE ON VENUS'S SURFACE?

Mountains cover about one-third of the planet. The tallest one, **Maxwell Montes,** is about 37,000 feet high. Compare this to the tallest mountain on Earth, Mt. Everest. It only stands about 29,000 feet high. Venus also has some very deep **canyons.** The deepest one extends down 9,500 feet!

3-D illustration of volcano Maat Mons on Venus

EARTH

There's no place like home. Is there, Pluto?

Earth is the third planet from the Sun. This position puts Earth in the solar system's "habitable zone." This area is far enough away from the Sun for liquid water to exist.

Earth is the only planet in our solar system that is known to support plant and animal life.

Earth from the surface of the moon

WHAT IS IN EARTH'S ATMOSPHERE?

Earth's atmosphere is made up of **nitrogen** (78%), oxygen (21%), and other gases (1%). Oxygen is what people need to breathe. **Carbon dioxide,** another gas, is released into the air naturally. It's also released when we burn coal, oil, and natural gas for fuel. Carbon dioxide traps the Sun's **heat** in Earth's atmosphere. As more carbon dioxide builds up, the planet gets hotter.

HOW FAST DOES EARTH MOVE?

It takes about 365 days—one year—for the Earth to circle the sun. Our planet moves at **66,000** miles an hour to make this trip! As it goes, it rotates on its axis. The planet spins at 11,000 miles per hour to do this. Each full **rotation** takes 24 hours—one day.

Meteor crater in Arizona

ARE THERE ANY CRATERS ON EARTH?

There sure are! Over billions of years, huge space rocks have smashed into the planet. They have left scars called **"impact craters."** The largest one we've found so far is the **Vredefort**

Crater in South Africa. Scientists think this 155-mile-wide crater is about 2 billion years old. Imagine the size of the space rock that made it! Most space rocks that enter Earth's atmosphere **burn up** before they reach the surface. Many have landed in the oceans.

MARS

Earth's other near neighbor, Mars, is about 142 million miles from the Sun. It is nicknamed the "Red Planet" because it's made mostly of metals and reddish-orange rock.

Gee, I thought one moon was great. Imagine having two!

The red color of Mars is actually just plain old rust! The rocks on Mars have a lot of iron in them. When it's exposed to oxygen, iron rusts and turns that reddish color.

Mars, taken by Viking orbiter

WHAT IS THE **AIR** LIKE ON MARS?

It's "gas-ly!" The air is 95% carbon dioxide, 3% **nitrogen,** and about 2% argon. The atmosphere looks pinkish orange because of all the **windstorms** that sweep up bits of **rusty dust!** These storms pack winds gusting up to 100 miles per hour. They can be small—covering an area of about 200 miles—or can cover the entire surface of the planet!

Olympus Mons on Mars

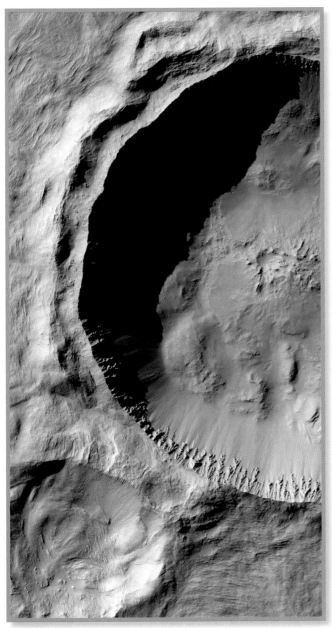

Gratteri Crater on Mars

WHAT IS THE **LANDSCAPE ON MARS** LIKE?

Mars has mountains, canyons, craters, and **volcanoes,** just like Venus and Earth. In fact, Mars is home to the largest volcano in the entire solar system, **Olympus Mons.** It towers 88,600 feet high and spreads 342 miles wide. The opening at the top is 50 miles across! Next to that, Earth's largest volcano, **Mauna Loa** in Hawaii, is practically a rabbit hole. It's only 33,476 feet high, 60 miles long, and 30 miles wide.

HOW MANY MOONS DOES MARS HAVE?

Mars has two moons, **Phobos** and **Deimos**. They have a weird shape, like lumpy potatoes! Earth's moon is 2,158 miles wide. Mars's moons are more like rocks in **comparison.** Phobos is only 14 miles wide, and Deimos is only 8 miles wide.

OUT OF THIS WORLD

Besides the planets, the Sun, and all the planetary moons, our solar system is home to a lot of interesting bodies in motion!

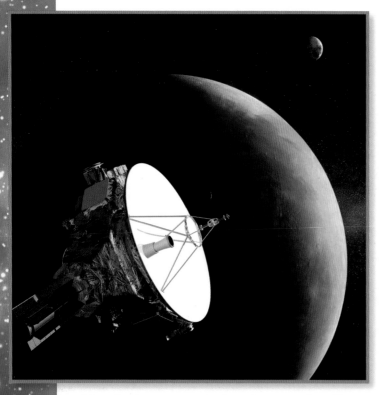

New Horizons spacecraft as it approaches Pluto (illustration)

HOW PLUTO BECAME A DWARF

In 1930, the scientific community declared there was a **ninth planet** orbiting the Sun and almost 3.7 billion miles from it. They called it Pluto. Then, in 2005, scientists discovered **Eris** orbiting the Sun far beyond Pluto. At 1,445 miles across, Eris is a little bigger than Pluto. Did that mean our solar system had ten planets? Instead of adding a planet, they decided to create a new category—**dwarf planet.** A "dwarf planet" is generally smaller than Mercury. It also has enough gravity to pull it into a round shape. A dwarf planet has other objects orbiting along with it—a planet doesn't. Both Eris and Pluto fit the description for a dwarf planet.

Asteroids approaching Earth (illustration)

NEAR-EARTH
OBJECTS

An asteroid or comet that passes close to Earth is called a **Near-Earth Object.** Asteroids—small, rocky objects with no atmosphere—orbit the Sun. Most of them—hundreds of thousands—occupy a circular belt between Mars and Jupiter. Some can reach 597 miles across! About once a year, an asteroid as big as a **car** enters Earth's atmosphere—but it burns up before it hits the ground. Comets are huge balls of frozen dust, gases, and rock. You've probably heard of **Halley's Comet.** It's visible about once every 75 years. It should come around again in July 2061—how old will you be then?

THE
KUIPER BELT

Pluto orbits the sun in the **Kuiper Belt,** a zone named after astronomer Gerard Kuiper. The Kuiper Belt begins near Neptune's orbit and extends almost 5 billion miles! This zone includes hundreds of thousands of **icy bodies**. Far beyond this is the mysterious Oort Cloud. It's said to contain countless *billions* of comets.

Object in Kuiper Belt (illustration)

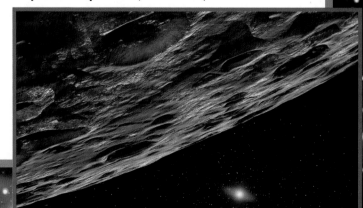

JUPITER

At 88,846 miles in diameter, Jupiter, the fifth planet from the Sun, is also the largest planet in our solar system.

Jupiter is one of four planets known as "gas giants." Jupiter, Saturn, Neptune, and Uranus are all balls of gas and liquid. They have little or no solid surface or core.

View of Jupiter from Pioneer spacecraft

WHY DOES JUPITER HAVE STRIPES?

The stripes we see across Jupiter are actually **layers of clouds**. The clouds are made up of all kinds of gases, including **ammonia**. That's why they're different colors. Some are even made up of **ice.**

Jupiter seen from its moon Europa (illustration)

Voyager 2 image of Great Red Spot

WHAT IS THE GIANT RED SPOT ON JUPITER?

It is a **gigantic,** swirling storm. It's called the **Great Red Spot** and has been raging for more than 300 years. Its winds have been clocked at over **270** miles per hour! The Great Red Spot may be just a "spot" on Jupiter, but it's about three times the size of Earth!

HOW MANY MOONS DOES JUPITER HAVE?

Jupiter has at least 62 moons. Many are record-setters. **Ganymede**—with a diameter of 3,273 miles—is the largest moon in our solar system. **Io** is home to the most active volcanoes in the solar system. **Callisto** has more craters than any other object in the solar system. **Europa** has an icy crust that covers an ocean. A moon is a lot like a planet, it just orbits something besides the Sun—in this case, Jupiter!

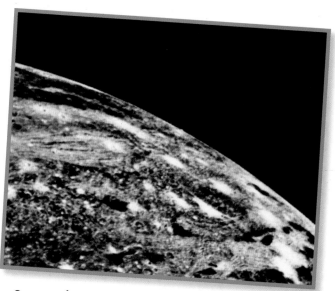

Ganymede

SATURN

Saturn, on average 891 million miles from the Sun, is the sixth planet in our solar system. At about 74,900 miles wide, it's also our second largest planet.

Saturn sure has a nice ring to it!

Saturn has nine major rings and thousands of smaller ones. These rings are made up of ice crystals, dust, and rock particles that can be as big as boulders!

Saturn viewed from one of its rings

WHAT'S IT LIKE ON SATURN?

Saturn is weird because its **gravity** is less than water. Because of this, Saturn would probably **float**—if you could find a bathtub big enough to drop it in!

Landscape on Hyperion, one of Saturn's moons (illustration)

Moon of Saturn

HOW MANY MOONS DOES SATURN HAVE?

Sixty-one and counting. **Titan,** the largest, is slightly bigger than Mercury. The only moon bigger is Jupiter's Ganymede.

Storm on Saturn's cloudy surface (illustration)

WHAT IS THE "WEATHER" LIKE ON SATURN?

Saturn has incredibly powerful storms with winds that can whip up to **1,000** miles an hour! These storms can produce **lightning strikes** a million times more powerful than those on Earth! They make Earth's **hurricanes** look like gentle breezes.

At its warmest, Saturn is about -190°F. But temperatures at the top of its clouds can drop to -300°F!

URANUS

Early astronomers could see only five planets: Mercury, Venus, Mars, Jupiter, and Saturn. In 1781, astronomer William Herschel used a telescope to peer into space. It revealed Uranus, the seventh planet in our solar system. And the coldest—brrr!

I think I found another planet!

The average temperature on Uranus is -371°F!

Illustration of Uranus and asteroids

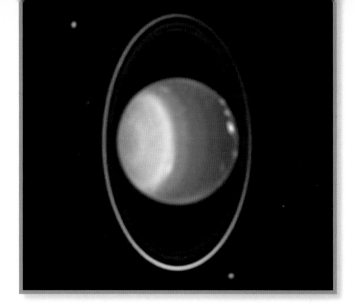

Uranus surrounded by its four major rings

WHAT KIND OF **ATMOSPHERE** DOES URANUS HAVE?

Uranus is mostly hydrogen (83%) and **helium** (15%), with traces of water and ammonia. But it also has methane (2%), which **absorbs** all the red in the light that reaches the planet. That's why Uranus looks **blue!**

HOW MANY MOONS DOES URANUS HAVE?

Scientists have found 27 moons orbiting Uranus. The largest, **Titania,** is about 980 miles wide. But some of Uranus's moons are as small as 8 miles! The moons closest to Uranus seem to be made of a **combination** of ice and rock. Titania and most of Uranus's other moons are named for characters from plays by William Shakespeare— including Cordelia, Cressida, **Juliet,** Ophelia, and Oberon.

WHAT IS UNIQUE ABOUT HOW URANUS **ROTATES?**

A planet usually tilts on its **axis**—the imaginary line running between its north to south poles. Jupiter and Venus tilt about 3 degrees each, and the Earth tilts about 23.5 degrees. But Uranus tilts **97.8 degrees**, so it rotates almost completely on its side! Scientists think that when it was young, Uranus had a **collision** with a very large space object about the size of Earth that knocked it sideways!

Uranus seen from the surface of its moon Cordelia (illustration)

NEPTUNE

Neptune, at 30,755 miles across, is the fourth largest planet in our solar system. It's also the farthest from the Sun at 2.8 billion miles away.

I thought Neptune was blue because it's so COLD!

Neptune is so far away from Earth, it is not visible in the sky.
Illustration of Neptune

WHAT WAS THE GREAT DARK SPOT? WHERE IS IT NOW?

In 1989, scientists noticed an oval-shaped "Great Dark Spot" on Neptune. It was a huge, **spinning storm** about the size of Earth. Its winds roared at 1,500 miles per hour! Scientists can't find the **Great Dark Spot** anymore. Did the storm **blow** itself out? Over the years, scientists have seen other storms appear and then fade out on Neptune.

Great Dark Spot

Wind streaks on Neptune's icy surface

Neptune, top left (illustration)

WHAT IS THE TEMPERATURE ON NEPTUNE?

Neptune sits about 30 times **farther** from the Sun than Earth, so it gets about one-thousandth of the sunlight and warmth. This makes Neptune's average temperature around **-366°F!** And like Uranus, the methane in Neptune's atmosphere **filters** out the red portion of light and makes the planet look blue.

HOW WINDY IS IT ON NEPTUNE?

Neptune has the fastest winds in the solar system—**1,200** miles an hour. That's more than five times faster than the **strongest winds** ever recorded on Earth!

Cygnus

Hercules

Canis Minor

LET'S DISCOVER
STARS

When you look up at the night sky, do
you see a few stars or a lot? No matter
how many stars you can see, billions
of them are up there. A star is actually
a big, glowing ball of gas! Stars shine
singly, in pairs, or as part of a pattern.

There are 88 star patterns—called
constellations—in our galaxy. Many
constellations are named after animals,
such as Ursa Minor ("Little Bear")
and Canis Minor ("Little Dog"). Other
constellations get their names from
Greek mythology, such as Perseus and
Hercules. These are just a few of the
exciting pictures the night sky draws
for you. Depending on where you live
and the season, the stars have a lot of
stories to tell!

Cassiopeia

Perseus

Pisces

Bootes

Ursa
Minor

Corona
Borealis

Virgo

Auriga

Aquila

THE SUN

The Sun plays a central, starring role in everything. No wonder—that's exactly what the Sun is, a star!

I could shine like the sun!

The Earth and all the planets in our solar system orbit around the Sun.

Illustration of planets orbiting the Sun

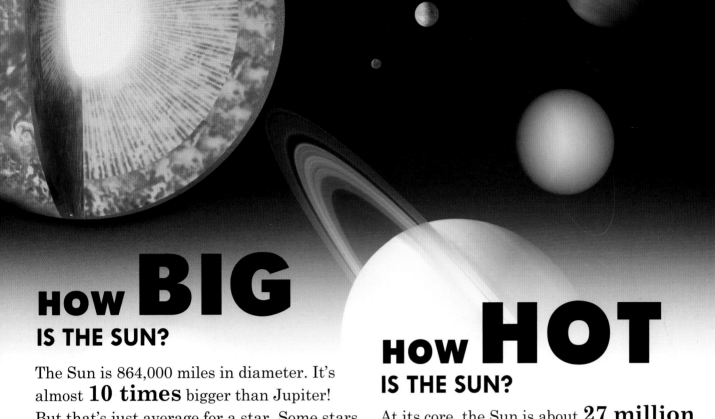

HOW **BIG**
IS THE SUN?

The Sun is 864,000 miles in diameter. It's almost **10 times** bigger than Jupiter! But that's just average for a star. Some stars are hundreds of times bigger!

Antares, in the constellation of Scorpius, is thought to be **700 times** bigger than our Sun. If the Sun were the size of a baseball, then Antares would be a globe measuring 134 feet across!

WHAT KIND OF **WEATHER** DOES THE SUN HAVE?

The Sun can experience huge **magnetic** storms. These "sunspots" break out on what passes for a surface on the gassy Sun—the **photosphere**. Sunspots can rage for several days or weeks. They are cooler than the rest of the photosphere. The number of sunspots goes up and down in an 11-year cycle.

Solar flares and solar **prominences** are stormy eruptions of gas that burst out of the photosphere at hundreds of miles per second. Flares can burn at 18 million degrees Fahrenheit! A prominence will hurl tons and tons of solar matter out into space.

HOW **HOT**
IS THE SUN?

At its core, the Sun is about **27 million** degrees Fahrenheit, more than 127,000 times hotter than **boiling** water! On the Sun's surface it is much cooler—"only" about 10,000°F.

The Sun has no surface since there's nothing **solid** to stand on. The Sun is a giant ball of **superhot gases** pressed together in layers.

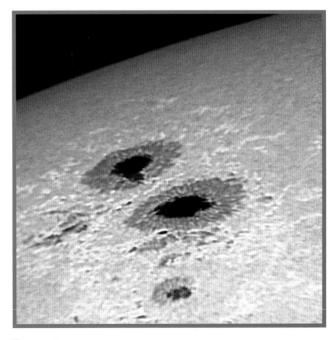

Sunspots

THE LIFE OF A STAR

The oldest stars in the sky have been around for about 13 billion years! But stars don't live forever.

I'm feeling hot enough to burn through Sulley's scare record tonight!

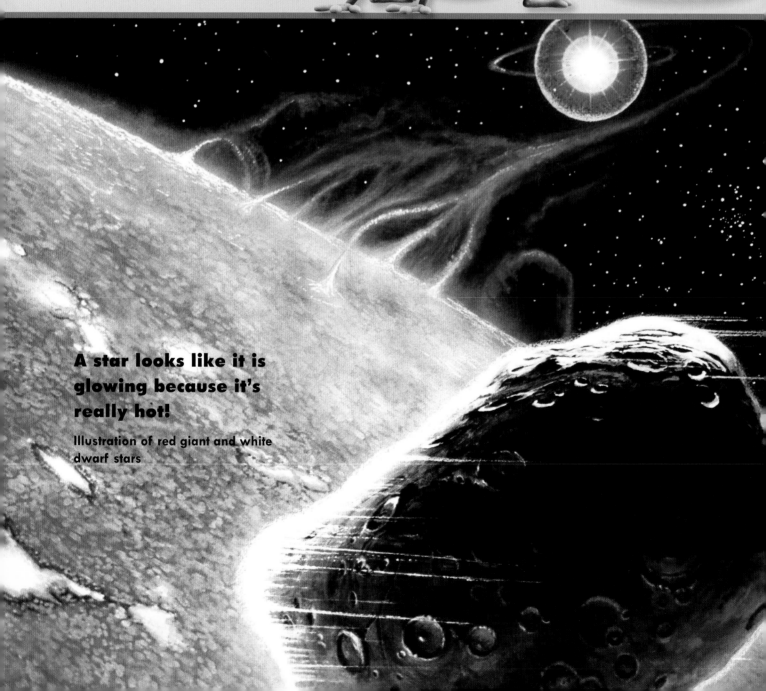

A star looks like it is glowing because it's really hot!

Illustration of red giant and white dwarf stars

HOW ARE STARS BORN?

A star is created inside a cloud of gas and dust called a **nebula.** The gas and dust are constantly moving. The whole mass spins faster and faster and **clumps** together tighter and tighter until it starts to **collapse** under its own weight. What's left is called a protostar. The center of a **protostar** heats up and eventually becomes a star.

Orion nebula star formation

Birth of a star

HOW DOES A STAR DIE?

As it runs out of **hydrogen fuel,** a star's core shrinks and gets hotter. The higher temperature makes the star grow bigger again. Then the outermost layers of the star cool and **burn off.** The entire star begins to glow red and stays a "red giant" for a few million years. Once a red giant has completely lost its outer layers, it becomes a much smaller star called a **white dwarf.** It takes billions more years for a white dwarf to cool off. Once it does, it reaches the final stage of death—a dark and cold black dwarf.

WHAT DIFFERENT COLORS CAN A STAR BE?

You can tell a star's temperature from its color. The very **hottest** stars are blue. Then, getting cooler as they go, comes blue-white, white, yellow-white, yellow, **orange,** and finally, red. Our Sun is a **yellow dwarf star** with a surface temperature about 10,000°F. A blue giant star can be 10 times hotter! A **red dwarf** is only about half as hot as our Sun.

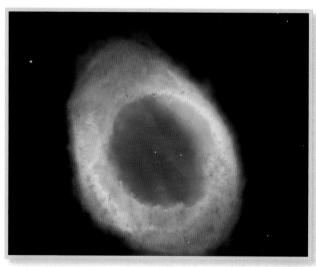

A dying star

BLACK HOLES

I can be scarier than a black hole!

Black holes are formed when stars or other massive objects collapse from their own gravity.

It's said that nothing can resist the pull of a black hole—not even light! That's why it's called a black hole.

Illustration of a star-sized black hole

Black hole

WHAT HAPPENS WHEN AN OBJECT GETS CLOSE TO A **BLACK HOLE?**

The black hole's force of gravity traps the object and pulls it ever closer. It's like a **vacuum cleaner** in space that sucks up anything that gets too close to it!

As an object nears the center of the hole, it tries to **resist** the hole's force. By the time the object arrives at the center of the hole, this struggle has given it a whole new shape—like a huge strand of spaghetti! No surprise then that scientists call this process the "noodle effect" or **"spaghettification."**

Supermassive black hole

COULD THE EARTH GET **SUCKED** INTO A **BLACK HOLE?**

Not likely. The closest black hole is still **trillions** of miles away from Earth. Scientists use a **mathematical** formula to figure out how close is too close to a black hole's pull. An object needs to cross the **"event horizon"** (the space around a black hole) to get trapped. Luckily, Earth is too far away from the closest black hole for us to worry about crossing the event horizon.

HOW POWERFUL IS A BLACK HOLE?

A black hole is the **strongest** force there is! It's like a **bottomless pit**—anything that falls inside it is never seen again. So we'll never know what the inside of a black hole looks like.

OUT OF THIS WORLD

After everything I ate today, I kind of feel like a ball of gas!

Everyone on Earth has gazed up at the sky. The stars have always held a grip on the human imagination.

Bright meteor and northern lights

WHAT YOU WISH UPON

The stars you wish on are actually **meteors!** Meteors start out as a piece of space debris or rock. **Debris** can range in size from a grain of sand to a boulder. When it enters the Earth's atmosphere, the meteor heats up and glows like a star. And meteors aren't just falling out of the sky; they're being pulled in by the Earth's **gravity.**

TWINKLE, TWINKLE

Everyone views stars with wonder and awe. But why do stars twinkle? They may seem to, but they really don't. It's an **optical illusion**—something that isn't what it looks like. The wind and particles in Earth's atmosphere are what's actually **moving.** This makes a **star** look to us like it's also moving—or "twinkling."

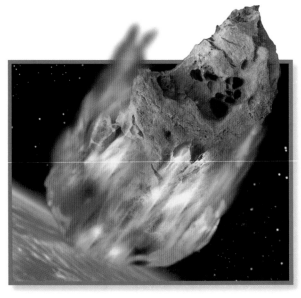

Meteor entering Earth's atmosphere (illustration)

MYTHS AND LEGENDS

Almost every major culture developed rich **folklore** about the Sun and stars. Ancient Egyptians presented the Sun as the **first god** (Ra or Re) who created the rest of the gods and the universe. In the Japanese religion of Shinto, it was a Sun goddess named **Amaterasu** who ruled heaven. She didn't get along with her brothers, one of whom was the god of the moon. It's why we have day and night—because they sit with their backs to each other!

In an ancient Chinese myth, ten Suns decided to shine at once. This killed all the crops on Earth and dried up all the water. Yi, an **archer,** had to shoot nine of the Suns, leaving only one.

Figure of Sun god in Egypt

A black hole

WE ARE ALL STARS

Some scientists think the same **elements** that make up stars make up everything in the universe. If that's the case, then we all have a little stardust in us!

CONSTELLATIONS

Ancient civilizations noticed that the stars formed patterns. Many cultures developed stories about these "pictures in the sky" called constellations.

That big clump of stars kind of looks like old Mr. Waternoose!

Everywhere you look in the night sky, you're sure to see a "story" in the stars.

Illustration of Ursa Minor

WHAT ARE SOME OF THE ANIMAL-SHAPED AND PEOPLE-SHAPED CONSTELLATIONS?

One of the largest constellations visible in the Northern Hemisphere is **Ursa Major,** which means the "Great Bear." According to Greek legend, Hera, the wife of Zeus, became jealous of **Callisto**, a nymph. Hera turned Callisto into a bear, but Zeus swept her and her son into the sky to keep them safe. Callisto's son is Ursa Minor, or the "Little Bear" constellation.

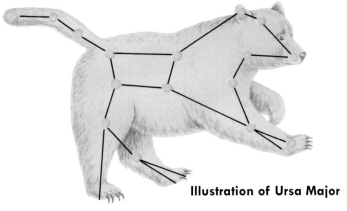

Illustration of Ursa Major

The constellation of **Orion** is named after the great hunter of Greek mythology. It is visible in winter in the Northern Hemisphere and in summer in the Southern Hemisphere. Orion's hunting dogs are in the sky with him. They are the constellations Canis Major ("Great Dog") and **Canis Minor** ("Little Dog").

Illustration of Canis Major

WHAT CONSTELLATIONS CAN YOU SEE?

That depends on where you are and what time of year it is. Some constellations are only visible in the **Northern Hemisphere;** others are only visible in the Southern Hemisphere. Some, like **Orion,** can be seen in both. And because Earth is always moving, you may not see the same **constellations** in fall and winter that you would in spring and summer.

GALAXIES

Our Sun shines brightly as the lone star in our solar system. But that doesn't mean our Sun lives by itself in space. Like any star, it belongs to a vast group of stars called a galaxy.

I've got to get Boo home even if I have to travel light years to do it!

As technology improves, so do scientists' calculations about how many galaxies there are.

Illustration of the Milky Way

The Milky Way

Milky Way over the Grand Canyon

WHAT GALAXY IS
OUR SUN A PART OF?

Our Sun—and our entire solar system—is part of the **Milky Way galaxy.** Every star you see in the night sky (there are about **400 billion** of them!) is part of the Milky Way.

HOW MANY
GALAXIES ARE THERE?

Scientists are still discovering galaxies, but they figure there are hundreds of **billions** of them! A single galaxy contains billions of stars. The **Triangulum galaxy** contains about 40 billion stars. That's about one-tenth as many as our own galaxy.

WHAT ELSE IS IN A
GALAXY BESIDES STARS?

A galaxy contains stars, **planets** that revolve around those stars, moons, comets, **asteroids,** and other objects, including a lot of gas and dust.

SPACE
OBSERVATION

People have always studied the skies, hoping to unlock the mysteries of space. As technology advanced, so did our ability to see objects that are millions of miles away. Today, over a dozen space probes send back images and information from outer space. Back here on Earth, observatories on every continent use high-powered telescopes and modern technology to find out what's going on all over the galaxy!

NORTH AMERICA

SOUTH AMERICA

EUROPE

ASIA

AFRICA

AUSTRALIA

ANTARCTICA

EARLY ASTRONOMY

The study of the universe is called astronomy. Without today's modern technologies, early astronomers relied on what they saw.

What's that? Oh, it's just my shadow. I'm like a sundial.

Before the telescope, scientists used mathematical calculations to figure out how the universe works.

Hubble telescope orbiting Earth

WHY DID PEOPLE BEGIN TO STUDY THE SKY?

The earliest **astronomers** were actually farmers and shepherds. They studied the sky to predict the changing of the seasons. Ancient Egyptians could tell by the movement of the stars when the Nile River would flood each year. They were able to figure out the right time to **harvest** their crops before the floods began.

An astrolabe

Stonehenge

WHAT KINDS OF **TOOLS** DID **ANCIENT PEOPLE** USE TO UNDERSTAND THE SKY?

The **astrolabe** is probably the oldest. It was invented in 150 BC! This instrument was used to **calculate** the position of the Sun and stars. In the 800s, the Arabic world developed it further and introduced it to Europe in the early 12th century. It became the most popular astronomical instrument until around 1650, when more **sophisticated** instruments replaced it.

WHAT WERE SOME OTHER ANCIENT WAYS TO TRACK THE SUN?

Different cultures had different tools to track the motion of the Sun and record days and seasons. The **sundial** is one of the oldest tools. People could tell time based on where shadows fell on it. **Stonehenge,** a ring of huge stones in southwest England, was probably arranged by ancient people to mark the **summer solstice**—the longest day of the year and the first day of summer. Stonehenge dates back to around 2400 BC.

A sundial

TELESCOPES

We can see faraway things up close with a telescope. Its invention in the early 1600s forever changed everything about astronomy and space from our point of view.

I can see clear to the kitchen!

Telescopes give us a view of our world and beyond!

Astronaut servicing Hubble Space Telescope

HOW CAN WE **SEE** **SPACE** FROM EARTH?

Astronomers place really high-powered **telescopes** far away from the bright lights of cities and other places with lots of people. The **Keck Observatory** sits on a dormant volcano on the U.S. island of Hawaii. Scientists from over 60 nations collaborated on the **Plateau Observatory.** It was built on the Antarctic Plateau at 13,000 feet above sea level. It's so cold there, the place is run by **robots!**

Death of a star from Chandra X-Ray Observatory

Nightfall from Keck telescope

HOW DO WE **SEE IN SPACE?**

The **Hubble Space Telescope,** the first optical space-based telescope, has orbited the Earth since 1990, looking for clues about our solar system. It moves at 17,500 miles an hour. It's huge, too—the size of a school bus—and as heavy as two male African elephants! The 45-foot long **Chandra X-Ray Observatory** was launched in 1999. It detects X-rays from **exploded** stars and has found a bunch of black holes across our galaxy.

WHAT WERE EARLY **TELESCOPES** USED FOR?

Early telescopes were often called **"spyglasses."** They were used by tradesmen to see ships carrying goods arriving in port. **Pirates** used them to spot ships at sea they could prey on. Telescopes also helped armies see where their enemies were in the field.

THE DAWN OF SPACE TRAVEL

Space is the place!

The "race to space" began in 1952. That's when an international space council recommended developing and launching satellites to map Earth's surface from space.

In 1954, scientists calculated that space would be buzzing with activity in the months between July 1957 and December 1958.

Satellite orbiting Earth

HOW MANY SATELLITES WERE LAUNCHED **BEFORE 1954?**

Satellite orbiting Earth

None. Several countries, including the U.S. and the Soviet Union, had only been developing **rockets.** Nothing had ever gone up that orbited the Earth. The council's idea was really expensive, but it would **revolutionize** space flight.

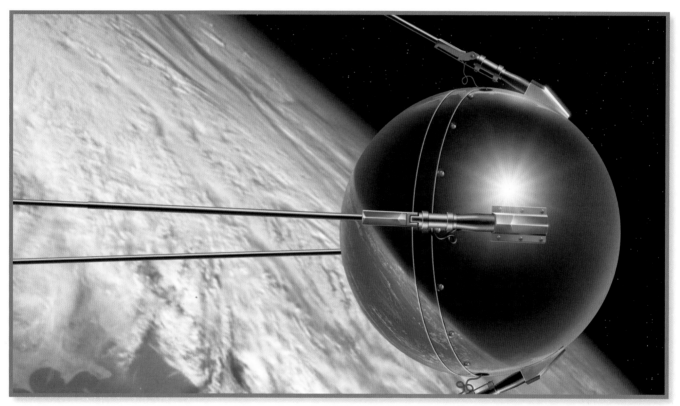
Sputnik 1 in orbit

WHAT WAS THE **FIRST SATELLITE IN ORBIT?**

The Soviet Union fired the first shot in the space exploration wars with **Sputnik 1,** launched on October 4, 1957. Sputnik 1 was tiny, when you think of a space ship—it was about the size of a **beach ball!**

It only weighed about 184 pounds. Sputnik 1 got to about 600 miles above the Earth. It **orbited** the planet every 96 minutes at speeds of up to 18,000 miles per hour! It fell back to Earth after three months. In January 1958, the U.S. sent **Explorer 1** into orbit. This satellite weighed almost 31 pounds. Explorer was 80 inches long and only 6.25 inches wide. It took 114.8 minutes to orbit the Earth.

EARLY SPACE TRAVELERS

Believe it or not, the first space travelers from Earth were actually animals! By sending animals into space, scientists were able to gain valuable information on how a living thing would function there.

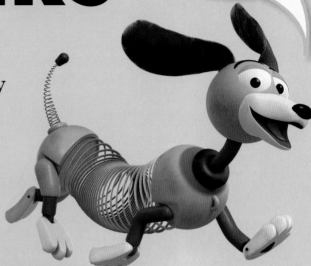

That brave dog sure was stretched to her limit!

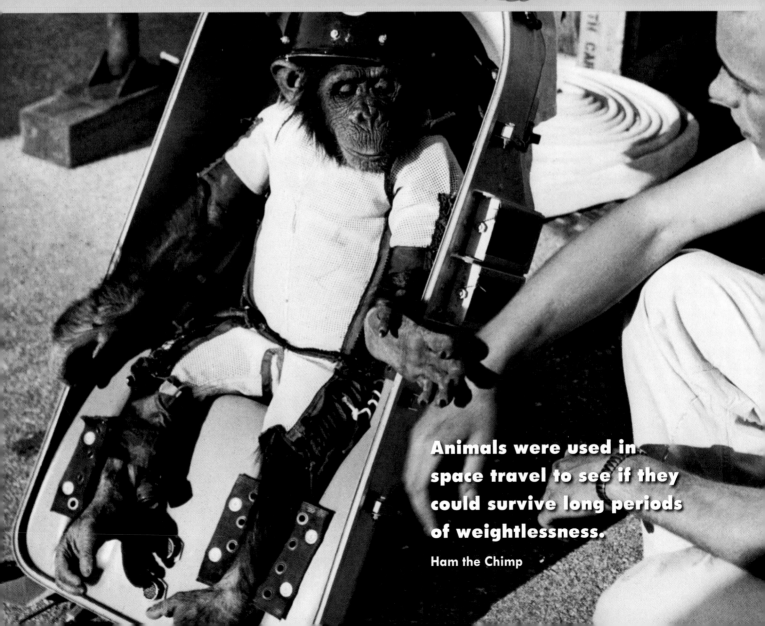

Animals were used in space travel to see if they could survive long periods of weightlessness.

Ham the Chimp

WHO WAS THE WORLD'S FIRST SPACE TRAVELER?

Before the U.S. launched **Explorer 1**, the **Soviet Union** sent a second satellite into orbit. This one carried a passenger—**Laika the dog!** Laika was a 13-pound stray. She had enough room to stand or lie down. Food and water were released at set times, and her waste was collected. The craft had enough **oxygen** for 10 days, but scientists figured the cabin got too hot, and poor, brave Laika died after only a day or two.

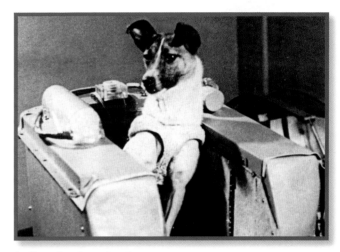

Laika, the first dog in space

Russian cosmonauts Aleksei Leonov (l) and Valeri Kubasov (r) boarding Soyuz 19

WHO WAS THE FIRST HUMAN SPACE TRAVELER?

Yuri Gagarin was the first person to orbit the Earth. On April 12, 1961, the Soviet Union launched **Vostok 1** for a 108-minute flight.

Aleksei Leonov of the Soviet Union was the first person to venture outside a spacecraft in orbit. The world's first **"Extravehicular Activity"** lasted for 20 minutes.

WHAT OTHER ANIMALS HAVE TRAVELED IN SPACE?

Many other animals have traveled to space since Laika. These include rabbits, turtles, insects, spiders, and **jellyfish.** The United States sent a number of monkeys and mice into space. On January 31, 1961, the U.S. sent up the world's first **chimpanzee.** Ham's flight only lasted for 16.5 minutes; he was **weightless** for less than a third of that time. Ham returned safely to Earth and lived for over 20 more years. **Felix,** the first cat into space, zoomed there in a French rocket in 1963. He successfully parachuted back to Earth in a capsule!

Yuri Gagarin

MAKING IT TO THE
MOON

The same year that people first orbited the Earth, U.S. President John F. Kennedy announced his country's goal to send people to the moon before the end of the decade. That goal was reached on July 20, 1969.

The first footprints made by astronauts on the moon are still there—there's no wind or water to blow them away, cover them over, or wear them down.

Americans reach the moon, 1971

WHAT KIND OF SPACE SUIT DID THE APOLLO ASTRONAUTS WEAR?

An Apollo astronaut's **space suit** was designed to meet all challenges. And, it was heavy! On Earth it weighed **180 pounds,** but up on the moon where there's no gravity, it only weighed about 30 pounds. An astronaut could keep cool, move around easily, and even go to the **bathroom!** A tube and bag system inside each suit collected waste, and the astronauts also wore special underwear that absorbed other waste products.

Crew of Apollo 11

Footprint on moon

WHEN DID ASTRONAUTS FIRST LAND ON THE MOON?

Anyone old enough to remember knows where they were on July 20, 1969—glued to a TV watching the world's first **moonwalk!** After leaving the Earth in the U.S. spacecraft Apollo 11, astronaut **Neil Armstrong** became the first person to step foot on the moon. He, **Buzz Aldrin** (who also walked on the moon) and Michael Collins (who stayed in orbit) took TV cameras along to share the historic moment with the world. As Armstrong stepped on the moon's surface, he said, "That's one small step for man, one **giant leap** for mankind."

HOW DID THE ASTRONAUTS GET TO THE MOON'S SURFACE?

The Apollo 11 spacecraft had different sections—or **modules**—to it. Besides the booster rockets that pushed it into space, it included a lunar landing module called the **Eagle.** Armstrong and Aldrin donned their space suits, hopped in the Eagle, and went down to the moon's surface.

The astronauts collected soil and moon rocks to bring back for study. They collected nearly 50 pounds of rock on that first moon landing! They also set up equipment to **observe** the moon after they returned to Earth.

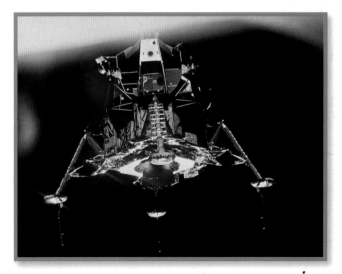

The Eagle

51

OUT OF THIS WORLD

Even though we've been there and back, the moon is still an object of fascination and is as big in our daily lives as it is in the sky. Let's find out some more about it!

Crater-pocked surface of the moon

MOON GLOW

The moon is the **brightest** object shining in the night sky. Only it isn't. The moon doesn't generate its own light. What we call "moonlight" is actually the sunlight **reflecting** off of it!

MEET THE **MOON**

On average, the moon is—whew!— **238,857** miles from Earth. It is 2,159 miles across, about two-thirds the size of Jupiter's Ganymede. Its name is simply **"the moon"** because, until Jupiter's moons were discovered, people thought it was the only one in our solar system.

IT'S GOING THROUGH **A PHASE**

As the moon **revolves** around the Earth, the amount of sunlight hitting its face changes. Each time you see a different amount of the moon, you are seeing another **phase.** A complete lunar cycle takes about 29.5 days. The cycle begins with the new moon—just a sliver is visible. From there the moon appears fuller and fuller. The time it takes to go from one new moon to the next is called a **lunation.** People have used this cycle to make calendars for as long as anyone can remember. A lunar calendar cave painting found in France may be 15,000 years old!

Lunar rover at the moon's Taurus-Littrow Valley

MOON ROCKS

During six **Apollo** missions to the moon between 1969 and 1972, U.S. astronauts brought back 2,200 samples of rocks, dust, sand, and pebbles. The samples weigh a total of **842 pounds**. Three unmanned Soviet spacecraft also came back with moon rocks. Scientists have studied the rocks to learn more about the moon, including its early history. They now think the moon could have been formed out of debris from a **collision** between Earth and an object as big as Mars!

Total lunar cycle

EXPLORING OUR SOLAR SYSTEM

Space programs around the world explore the moon and other objects in space. Unmanned space probes send back information, adding to what we know about our solar system.

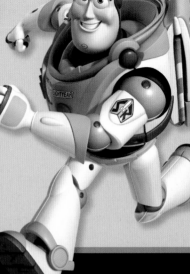

I've been to all the planets and all around the entire galaxy!

Unmanned probes have traveled to all seven of the other planets and visited comets and asteroids, too.

Sputnik 1 with moon

WHAT WERE THE **FIRST PROBES** TO STUDY OTHER PLANETS?

When the United States probe **Mariner 2** flew past Venus on December 14, 1962, it became the first probe to study another planet. It **scanned** Venus's atmosphere and surface and sent back information about Venus's rotation, its temperature, and other information.

In 1965, **Mariner 4** was the first probe to send back a photo of Mars showing the red planet's cratered, moonlike surface.

The first probe to **orbit** another planet was Mariner 9 in 1971. It circled Mars, sending back photos of 20 volcanoes.

Mariner 4

HAVE PROBES EVER DISCOVERED **ALIENS?**

Not yet! But the **Pioneer** and Voyager probes carry information from Earth in case they should encounter alien life forms. Each Pioneer probe has a **plaque** showing a man and a woman and a diagram showing where the Earth sits in the galaxy. Each Voyager spacecraft has a gold-plated copper disk. These hold recordings of sounds and images that show the **diversity** of life on Earth!

Pioneer 10 (illustration)

Image of the surface of Mars

INTERNATIONAL SPACE STATION

This ship is out of this world!

The International Space Station, a collaboration of 16 countries, has been a unique workplace and home for astronauts since 2000. The ISS measures 356 feet from end to end and weighs almost 1 million pounds!

The ISS is constantly orbiting the Earth. By its 10th anniversary, the ISS had logged more than 1.5 billion miles!

International Space Station (ISS) from Endeavour

HOW DID SOMETHING THAT **BIG** GET INTO SPACE?

It was launched in parts—or modules—and then **assembled** in space! The first parts were put together in 1998. The whole thing was completed over 13 years. More than 100 parts make up the ISS. Each participating nation also contributed some of the major components. The **Columbus Laboratory,** a place where scientists conduct research in physics and life sciences, was contributed by the European Space Agency.

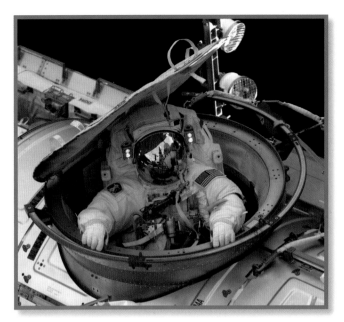

Space shuttle Endeavour on last trip to ISS

NASA prepares for launch of space shuttle Atlantis

HOW DO PEOPLE AND THINGS GET TO **THE ISS?**

There actually is a fleet of **shuttle buses** available to take astronauts and supplies back and forth between Earth and the ISS! They can travel either by the European Space Agency's **automated** transfer vehicle, or via Russian Soyuz or Progress **spacecraft.** The first crew stayed for almost 5 months. Some later crews have stayed aboard for closer to 6 months.

WHAT DO ASTRONAUTS **RESEARCH** AT THE ISS?

Astronauts research **space's environment** and how it affects living things. In 10 years, astronauts aboard the ISS had conducted more than 600 **experiments!**

International Space Station crew

LIFE IN THE INTERNATIONAL SPACE STATION

Have you ever wondered what it would be like to live in the ISS? For starters, up to six astronauts can live there at any time.

Say, is there room for one more?

The living area of the ISS is as big as a five-bedroom house in the United States.
Crew of space shuttle Discovery

WHY DO ASTRONAUTS NEED TO **EXERCISE IN SPACE?**

The lack of **gravity** in the ISS causes bones to **weaken** since they aren't needed to support a body's weight. So exercise is necessary when you live aboard. The astronauts are **harnessed** to the **exercise** equipment so they won't **float** away!

Lunch onboard Discovery, 1985

HOW DO ASTRONAUTS GO TO THE **BATHROOM** IN THE ISS?

A regular **toilet** won't work because the lack of **gravity** won't keep things flowing in the right direction. Machines onboard use **suction** to help remove and store waste.

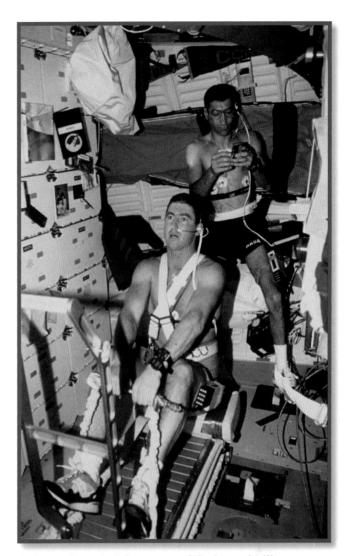

Astronauts exercising on modified treadmill

WHAT DO ASTRONAUTS **EAT IN THE ISS?**

There is no **refrigerator,** so they eat a lot of canned or packaged food. They also eat **dehydrated** food (just add water), bread, dried fruits, and nuts. There is juice, tea, coffee, milk, and water. The astronauts have to drink through a **straw.** When a new shuttle arrives, it delivers fresh fruits and vegetables.

Water is an extremely valuable but limited resource on board the ISS. Everything that is a liquid is recycled—that includes the urine, spit, and **sweat** of all the crew members and laboratory animals!

PLANETARY FACTS

JUPITER
1 Orbit of the Sun: 4332.59 days
1 Rotation: 9 hours, 55 minutes
Distance from Sun: 483 million miles
Average Temperature: -244°F
Atmosphere: hydrogen, helium,
    methane
Diameter: 88,846 miles

MARS
1 Orbit of the Sun: 686.98 days
1 Rotation: 24 hours, 37 minutes
Distance from Sun: 142 million miles
Maximum Temperature: 98°F
Minimum Temperature: -190°F
Atmosphere: carbon dioxide, nitrogen,
    argon
Diameter: 4,222 miles

VENUS
1 Orbit of Sun: 224.701 Days
Distance from Sun: 67 million miles
Average Temperature: 850°F
Atmosphere: carbon dioxide,
    nitrogen
Diameter: 7,523 miles

EARTH
1 Orbit of Sun: 365.3 days
Distance from Sun: 93 million miles
Average Temperature: 45°F
Atmosphere: nitrogen, oxygen,
    argon
Diameter: 7,926 miles

MERCURY
1 Orbit of Sun: 87.969 Days
Distance from Sun: 36 million miles
Maximum Temperature: 870°F
Minimum Temperature: -300°F
Atmosphere: hydrogen, helium
Diameter: 3,030 miles

URANUS
1 Orbit of the Sun: 30,684 days
1 Rotation: 17.2 hours
Distance from Sun: 1.8 billion miles
Average Temperature: -300°F
Atmosphere: hydrogen, helium,
   methane
Diameter: 31,763 miles

NEPTUNE
1 Orbit of the Sun: 60,190 days
1 Rotation: 16 hours, 17 minutes
Distance from Sun: 2.8 billion miles
Average Temperature: -366°F
Atmosphere: hydrogen, helium,
   methane
Diameter: 30,775 miles

SATURN
1 Orbit of the Sun: 10,759.2 days
1 Rotation: 10 hours, 13 minutes
Distance from Sun: 891 million miles
Average Temperature: -300°F
Atmosphere: hydrogen, helium,
   methane
Diameter: 74,898 miles

GLOSSARY

asteroid: a small, irregularly shaped object with no atmosphere that orbits around our Sun

astrolabe: equipment from ancient times used to observe the Sun and other stars

astronomy: the study of celestial objects, space, and the universe

atmosphere: a mixture of gases surrounding the Earth and other planets

axis: an imaginary straight line running from north to south through a planet

black dwarf: what a small or medium star becomes when it dies

comet: a clump of frozen gas and dust that is heated to the point of glowing as it approaches the Sun

constellation: a group of stars forming a recognizable pattern or a "picture in the sky"

core: innermost layer of the Sun or a planet

crater: indentations created on the surface of a planet or moon from the impact of an asteroid or a comet smashing into or against the surface

dwarf planet: a celestial body that is generally smaller than Mercury, has enough gravity to pull it into a round shape, and has other objects orbiting in its path

event horizon: the surface of a black hole

galaxy: a grouping of millions or billions of stars and their solar systems, if any, and moons, comets, asteroids, other space objects, and debris

gravity: an invisible force that pulls objects toward one another

greenhouse effect: when carbon dioxide gas traps the Sun's heat near the planet's surface and prevents it from leaving

light year: a measure of vast distance, about 5.9 trillion miles

meteor: the streak of light caused by a meteoroid as it rushes through Earth's atmosphere

meteoroid: a piece of space debris or rock ranging in size from a grain of sand to a boulder

nebula: a cloud of gas and dust in which stars are born

observatory: a building from which people observe the stars and the sky, usually with the use of powerful telescopes

orbit: the path a celestial body takes around a center of attraction or another celestial body

photosphere: a layer of the Sun's atmosphere located above the core and below the chromospheres

planet: an object in orbit around the Sun large enough to have its own gravity

protostar: an early stage of a star, before it heats up and begins burning fuel

satellite: a manmade spacecraft that orbits the Earth

solar flare: an sudden eruption of intense, high-energy radiation from the surface of the Sun

solar prominence: an eruption of hydrogen that can rise for tens of thousands of miles off of the Sun

solar system: a collection of planets, their moons, and smaller bodies (stars, asteroids, meteoroids, comets) in orbit around a star

space probe: an unmanned spacecraft traveling through space and sending back information for scientists to study

spaghettification: the process by which an object changes into a long, thin shape as it approaches the center of a black hole

star: a ball of gas that appears to glow from the burning of hydrogen

star cluster: a group of stars

Sun: the star at the center of our solar system

sundial: an instrument that helps people to tell the time of day based on where shadows fall on it

telescope: a device that makes distant objects look closer and larger

universe: everything that exists

INDEX

PHOTO CREDITS